THE GREAT BLUES

Steven H. Semken

Illustrations
Andrew R. Driscoll

Woodley Memorial Press
Washburn University
Topeka, Kansas

The Great Blues

©2005 Steven H. Semken
illustrations ©2005 Andrew R. Driscoll

ISBN 0-939391-36-8

First Edition (revised 1st edition, Feb. 2006)

Woodley Press Collection
The Bob Woodley Memorial Press
Washburn University, Topeka, KS 66621
(785) 231-1010 ext. 1735
www.washburn.edu/reference/woodley-press

Manufactured in the United States of America

The paper used in this publication meets the minimum requirements of the American National Standard for Information Sciences—Permanence of Paper for Printed Library Materials, ANSI Z39.48-1992

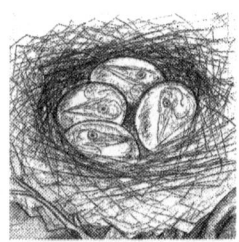

Nothing seems to arrive as easily as expected in the realm of the written word, there are always many acts of generosity and just as many hills of persistence that need to be overcome. Any faults, misprints, slights of hand are mine. First off, I wish to thank Andy Driscoll; alas, our *moment* of gas station enlightenment proved worthy. Thank you to Denise Low & Paul Fecteau at Woodley Press. Thanks also to Wes Jackson, Mary Swander & Robert Butler for encouragement and words beyond the call of duty and also to Annie Grieshop for additional edit work & as always, wingfullflights of lovingkindness to my fulltime valentines Laura & Fenna!—SSemken

"To those devoid of
imagination a blank
place on the map is
a useless waste;
to others, the most
valuable part"
—Aldo Leopold

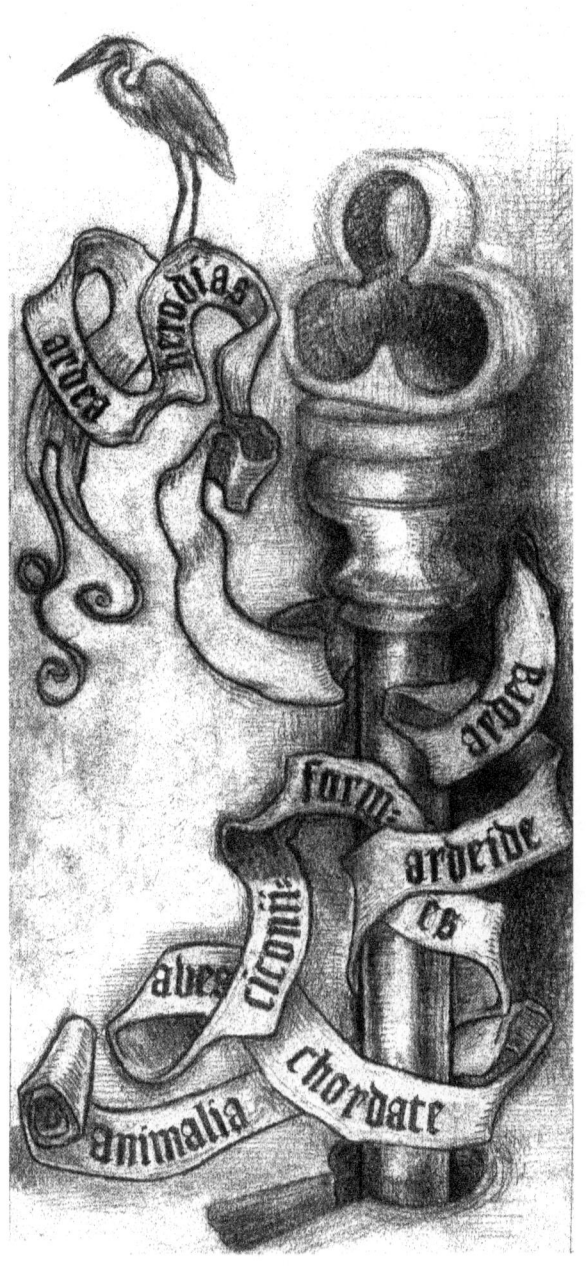

*"Reassured by our indifference other
creatures may come calling, asking
who we are, ready to visit."*
—Gary Holthaus

Preface—Hints

The only thing necessary was a shard of evidence. I needed some tiny hint or clue to reveal what was happening, needed something turned in my imaginary favor to tilt and better explain the magical amalgam so coiled in my head as I sat, gawking and marveling, during my first excursion to a rookery of Great Blue Herons. I wanted some proof that the birds and their habitat were real.

Following the rough directions given me from a friend, I journeyed to a spot so well concealed and safe, I trembled with the feeling of immensity. My grip on sanity and reality was erased as soon as I arrived. I became frazzled and lost as above me drifted ninety, perhaps more than a hundred Great Blue Herons. They were so close I could hear their wings flap. When I first arrived, maybe fifty of them rose and flew in different directions then slowly, slowly they each relaxed in my presence and resettled on their nests. At one time or another, though, there were at least fifteen or so of the birds, rising, flying, leaving, coming from a nest.

As I watched, entirely captivated, these tall birds engaged themselves in a multitude of activities. Some were perched on the limbs of the tall, old-growth sycamore trees. Others landed on the earth to stare at the creek water, while others circled wide and high overhead. Watching them, my eyes were busy darting back and forth, so quickly I actually may have hypnotized myself. I couldn't believe that I even gazed at a couple of the birds puffing out their plume feathers and then in utter amazement I watched as each of them wrapped their wings around themselves as though dressing in robes. I was so enamored, so intrigued it wouldn't have surprised me if I had looked up and seen a herd of Herons hanging upside down in the trees like giant bats.

I observed the males offering their female companions sticks to build nests. After the initial shock from the variety of movements, I noticed the small heads of baby Herons just above the rim of nests, and then, lightly, I made out the lightest peeps of these babies calling for food. Such hospitality and trust before me. I wondered if I had been invited, or was intruding. Either way my blood was rushing and my mind was racing. There was no question, I had truly found the center of the world, here, in an isolated corner of northeastern Kansas.

These great blue birds and their hermitic habits merged with all my preconceived notions about dreams and reality, hopes and fears. No clear detail stands out as the cause for my sudden infatuation. Perhaps it was the odor of wild mushrooms and guano in the air, the piles of pale white bone strewn on the ground amongst the leaves and branches of the sycamore trees hosting the Heron nests. Perhaps it was the eerie variety of clacking, squalling and barking sounds I could distinguish coming from the Heron's long curved necks? I do remember laughing to myself, remembering I used to think the Great Blue Heron couldn't make noises. I observed and listened. There were clearly as many as fourteen different Heron noises being released around me.

I was charmed as well as frightened by their wildness. I wondered if the Heron's peering yellow eyes were able to see through to my deepest thoughts. Perhaps the birds knew I would be scared to feel the texture of their feathers if any of them were to land next to me without warning, knew that I would scream and my heart would drop to my ankles if one of them quickly locked its gaze upon me. Maybe they were aware that if they stuck out their long necks and released a loud bark, I'd probably run away and never come back. At the same time, torn between fantasy and reality, I desperately wanted to touch these semi-reptilian birds. I truly wanted to smell their breath and feel the draft of air coming from the flapping of their wings.

A craving stirred in my stomach—some elemental, alchemical combination was being presented for me to understand. I thought of a passage in Richard Nelson's book *An Island Within* when he retells the formula for a good hunter: "A good hunter…that's someone the animals *come* to." This comment made me think: What makes a good bird watcher? Easy, someone the birds let *see* them. Why, I wondered, were the Great Blue Herons of Kansas offering themselves to me? What had I done to get so close to these creatures? I was standing right beside their nests; they were letting me watch their mating rituals and yet they seemed unashamed before me. I felt certain I was being offered a wildly crazed, prehistoric blessing.

I lost track of sensibility. Having gawked at their behaviors, I felt as though I were slowly sinking into the earth and more connected with this place in Kansas than I had ever felt connected with anything before. After I left this rookery for the first time, I was simply crazed with all things Heron. People questioned my extreme attraction to this mysterious, winged creature. Some were even embarrassed at my diligence. I watched for hours the movement of Herons along the Kaw River. I rushed to the shoreline with plaster of paris to make molds of their footprints. I scooped up the sand they had walked in and sniffed it, a few times, late in the evening, hoping to merge with sunset's long shadows. I even rubbed their droppings on my chest and tried to imitate the half bark-half belching noise they make when startled and lift away in quick flight, "FRahhhawwwk!"

Over the next fourteen years I remained stumped, trying to figure out how to explore and come to terms with these Great Blues and this spot on earth, which I knew to be the center of the world. I never questioned my need to examine and explore. Mircea Eliades wrote, "The discovery or projection of a fixed point—the center—is equivalent to the creation of the world."

Over time though I feared my thoughts were becoming too frenetic, too far-fetched, too beyond control. All my searching and wondering I hoped would not drive me into disarray. Abstraction and too much thinking, I knew, could lead to an oblique and cratered fantasy until I would be unable to tell anyone much more than a mumbling, jumble of eclectic philosophical, psycho-spiritual hogwash. All the same, though, I was beginning to believe in new ways of knowing, and there was no question that the deep woods held some supernatural, high energy elixir of truth to which I had been given access. I knew it was strange, but mixing creek water with Heron feathers and sycamore seed balls was a definite serum of truth I enjoyed sipping. I had gulped down what must certainly be a remedy of place-based, sympathetic magic.

I can't lie though. My wife did not understand my strains and consternations. She told me, quite matter of factly, I was absolutely making things too hard, "After all," she declared, "aren't you just writing about a bunch of birds in the woods?" Aghast at even the suggestion that my obsessions were trivial, I quickly pointed out that a "bunch" of Great Blue Herons should properly be referred to as a "siege" of Herons. My comment merely served my own intentions, since I was the only one who knew this tidbit of knowledge. I intended my remark to demonstrate the difficult and beseeching conflicts so obviously placed before me. It was clear that my wife did not share my struggles. I was certain, though, that given enough time, I would stumble upon, figure out, or at least come to terms with this rookery and the ever-tightening clench the twigs and feathers and trees of the Herons' habitat had on my brain.

What I hoped would happen is that my searching would allow me to discover some little-known detail of the natural world. I was convinced I had entered a realm of pure discovery and was at the core of some long misunderstood and forgotten myth. Rousseau once wrote, "It is on the summits of mountains, in the depths of the forest, or desert islands that nature reveals her most potent charms," with which I agree whole-heartedly. In my opinion, I had been placed under a potent charm. I needed only to learn to observe and decipher.

Then, about a year ago, visiting the rookery for the umpteenth time, it crossed my mind that maybe my wife was right. This was just a story about some birds in some trees along a creek edged with giant cottonwood and sycamore trees! This thought allowed my problems in understanding this rookery to be mine, not the Herons', not the trees', not the water's. I was close to believing this, but even as I became more comfortable with this thought, there seemed to be some sort of a blind spot forming in my upper cortex, attached to my very nerve endings, which just would not move and continued to nag on the edges of my possible certainty. There was one crucial detail being overlooked and I hit upon the clue in a short verse of poetry by W.S. Merwin:

> *I want to tell what the forests*
> *were like*
> *I will have to speak*
> *in a forgotten language*

After reading these words, a vague and seldom-utilized portion of my instinctual brain began tocking. A subtle change whirled through my lungs and sternum, back outside my mouth and spread across the expansive space of prairie before me. I thought of how the land brings birth to all things. Of course, of course, of course there was a truth older than words being spoken by these Herons that I needed to understand.

I had once read about the human brain being three layers deep, the oldest being the "reptilian," the second the "neo-mammalian." The third layer, the "neo-cortex" is the newest and is a thin crust covering the other two layers of the brain. I was hopeful I could dig around in my old, reptilian brain cells where archetypes, as well as ancient hunting and gathering instincts were swirling. I just needed one tiny hint, one tiny shard of evidence that I could find my way into these old, old thoughts.

ii.

I started my day intent on visiting the rather grotesque set of sculptures in Lucas, Kansas, known as the *Garden of Eden*. While heading southeast from the Black Hills and the beautiful mounds of earth of the Badlands, I decided to stop in the unincorporated village of Round Rock, Kansas, nestled up alongside the slumbering flow of the South Fork of the Solomon River. I was in need of a quick rest. Pulling in to the center of the village, I was pleased and a bit surprised to spot a used book store. Enjoying the smell of old paper and being a collector of regional-based, natural history essays and odd, local short stories, I was excited at the chance to browse this off-the-beaten-trail location.

Stepping out of my car, I felt the prairie wind that bounced and rattled the metal signs around me. Recalling my friend Dewmore Max's comment with a sly grin—"Wind only blows around here twice a year, six months from the south, six months from the north." I gave a quick shake of my head and stretched my back and travel weary legs until I could feel my lower spine pop. I looked off to the distance at a line of high and heaven-reaching cumulonimbus clouds in the Southwestern sky.

Entering the *Scratch Pad Bookstore* I heard a faint, but friendly, "Hello" emerge from what looked to be a middle-aged man, his face deeply buried in an old issue of a numerology magazine. He would occasionally spin in his chair, shovel a spoonful of breakfast cereal into his mouth, whilst uttering numerical values under his breath. He seemed entirely uninterested in my arrival. There was no music, no television being played, and the store was entirely silent except for the store keeper's mumbling about prime numbers and the value of one. After some browsing I discovered a fascinating publication, which in all my searches for writings on Herons, I had never encountered: *Nesting Habits & Ornithological Constellations of the Great Blue Herons in the Mid-Prairie Regions* (Holiseventh Press, Lawrence, Kansas, 1933), authored by Dr. Horatio Flatstone, Department of Ornithology and Comparative Literature at what I knew was the now-defunct Nemaha State University, once considered the pinnacle of higher education in the midst of the Flint Hills.

I pulled the publication off the shelf and noticed that the entire manuscript had yet to be trimmed along the outer edges. Without any consideration of price, I made my way to the front of the store, quickly paying whatever amount the shopkeeper told me. Exiting the front door in a befuddled and anxious state of mind, I raced outside. Standing beside the front door of my car, I felt my breath return. I looked over and noticed a picnic table and my heart slowed down. I walked over to the table, from which I could see and hear the Solomon River, sat down and began reading.

The small publication was crammed full of revelations, significantly aiding my years of premonitions on the evolution and lore Great Blue Heron. I suppose I should add I entirely forgot about the *Garden of Eden* that day. Instead, I spent the remainder of the day reading my newly-found publication with a passion no book had previously provided me. The reading was fairly dense and not entirely straightforward but laced with metaphors and unconventional conclusions. As I read along, I had to slice open each new page with my pocketknife. I was entirely engrossed in the reading. If a tornado had ripped right through during those next few hours of reading I wouldn't have noticed.

Upon finishing the book I looked around and saw three or four Great Blues flying overhead as the sun went down. I returned to my car and raced down the highway toward my home in Viriditas, Kansas, near the Leavenworth and Jefferson county line. I needed to go to the rookery and pay attention to a hollow, old sycamore tree I had passed on my walks to the birds. This giant tree had always caught my attention, but now I was beginning to understand why.

"He may have to steer his way home through
the dark by the north star, and he will feel
himself to some degrees nearer the star for
having lost his way on the earth."
—Henry D. Thoreau,
Natural History of Massachusetts

2. Introduction—Ages Ago

On a silent spring evening during the Miocene, some four-teen million years ago, amidst the bloom of hardy woodland flowers, what appeared to be a constellation of great blue herons begun forming in the northern sky. Great Blues were being hurled out of the dense middle of the earth, one by one, through the hollowed trunk of a giant sycamore tree. Bird after bird heaved in tight and curled-up fashion where they became visible against the backdrop of the Milky Way. This release of birds went on eighteen hours without inter-ruption. Each bird was slightly different from another, just as every wind that blows is an entirely unique movement. Some Great Blues had blotches of crimson on their bills, others long white plume feathers. Still others were glossed in pow-dery layers of fossilized sea salt.

Having been concocted in alchemical fashion through the fusion of earthly elements—way down in darkness where gold is believed to form and congeal and develop ever so slowly—the Great Blue Herons were being released from out

of the earth to embark upon a journey that would involve living in a sacred realm: just above the ground, very next to clouds, in sight of the sun, resting on a pillow of invisible air amidst the tips of tree branches and the soft cushion of river bed. One can hardly turn these birds into angels, but there is no doubt they live in the third realm of the spheres, in a spot where they can hear and see the Gods as they move around within the manifested, physical world. Their initial mission was, as Aristotle the ancient Greek might have proclaimed, "to go and live in a state of perfect being."

As with anything deemed perfect, however, there was no more than an instant of paradise in the air once the thin and wispy Herons reached the Milky Way. Granted, this all happened so long ago there is no way to know for certain how the night sky looked that evening*, but one has to imagine that the Herons glowed in a magnificent pattern, blazing with their long necks curled tight, poised ready to bark out loud and fly. Their constellation persisted just one night and one night only before the Great Blues took flight and glided neither further up in the sky, nor back into the depths of the earth, but instead took roost on the surface of the earth, procreating in the tips of the highest trees, taking food from out of the ripples of mud and water, even devouring small rodents.

*Efforts to capture, or perhaps, recapture the arrival of the light from this constellation, via the speed of light, will no doubt be of interest to many, those studying the birds, as well as those obscure, yet serious, astronomers who allow themselves to believe in "momentary" constellations.

The Herons understood that to remain up in the sky was too "perfect." Living as mere twinkles, millions of light years away from the earth, would provide an uninteresting and continuous blandness.

Paul Shepard writes that "perfection insinuates a cloying monotony." Considering the habitat of the Great Blue Heron and their habits of isolation, to be left on display in the night sky would never have satisfied their reclusive instincts. One has to imagine a couple of things. Being placed in a static position would have been unbearable for a creature that wants to fly. Secondly, the Great Blues much prefer to be tiny dots upon the surface of a single planet of the universe, resting and nesting atop a sycamore tree in a long forgotten, buggy midland valley, not on display day and night to whomever and whatever is being served nighttime in this universe of ours.

Although no device has been created to verify the Herons' birth so many years ago, there are still ways to explain their origin. Being present is not such an obstacle as it may appear. Scientific theory has been able to explain, as have stories and rationalizations, many occurrences in the natural world. In the book by Dr. Horatio Flatstone, many points are used to explain the origin of the Herons. For instance, the universality of the *Emerald Tablet* refers to the birds, "Ascending from earth to Heaven, and then descending to earth again."

Perhaps this piece of wisdom seems a bit full of mysticism, yet the world does, even after the examinations of the most precise and carefully known documents of science, offer no clear understanding of itself. It is rather common knowledge now that the world ultimately boils down to having faith in the unknown, not in clinging to what little we think we know. Albert Camus once stated something along the lines of, "Science that was to teach me everything ends up in a hypothesis." In the whispering, reverent environment of the rookery, this statement can mean no more, no less than needing faith that these wide-winged species emerged as much from the air as from the soil, as much from fire as from water and in the end needing the bond of spirit.

Horatio is not alone in these thoughts of the Great Blues coming from out of the center of the earth. Others have said as much in various ways. The need for "reasonable intuition" has always been used as a manner of understanding and thought. A small line from Samuel Butler goes, "All reason is against it, and all healthy instinct is for it." Without doubt, I cannot recall how often this comment of Mr. Butler's has crossed my mind during my quest to know the Great Blues. I can only imagine that it must have influenced Horatio as well.

Dr. Flatstone's publication aptly points out, "We know that of the Great Blue Heron (*Ardea herodias*) there consists in structure and attitude equal amounts of both earth and sky." Perhaps a few passages from the doctor's book will better acquaint the reader with this idea:

> —Evidence clearly indicates that a thin and hollow wishbone was broken, precisely and exactly in half during a tug between the inner sphere of the earth and the outer orb of the sky. The result of which sent these large, grayish blue birds of a prehistoric, reptilian appearance to the surface of the earth where they have since existed in the wildest of areas: not only within isolated habitats, but even detached from their own shadows

for days and months at a time. The bird, an entirely natural creature, lives alone within its own species as often as possible. Mating season entices the large bird uncharacteristically out of its usual behavior as it barks and kaws and flies in unique ways.

—These forty-to-fifty-inch-tall birds bear their wildness, perhaps unjustly, with tightly coiled necks. The column of neck vertebrae is tightly curved in a double folded (S) shape. These bones are interlocked in folds and cusps skillfully held together with unique tendons, allowing the neck to move quickly forward, but just as importantly, providing the neck with unusually strong power so that it may spring back into a tight position with food in grasp. Almost immediately, they are once again ready to strike out for the gifts offered during the search for food.

—Their necks appear bound at all times, except when straining to show off their strength during mating season. At that time, the males push their necks out painfully straight, as though in victory over gravity, proceeding to fly in large oblong loops, displaying both courage and agility in order to win the approval of an admiring, yet not completely convinced female. The strength (not to mention the sheer necessity of clear, wide open space) needed to perform this demonstration of commitment has proved a useful talent and if interpreted properly by the female enables the reproduction of the species to proceed.

—Each epoch of time is definite in what it produces. The development during the Miocene is that of the grassland with the arrival of the large mountains in the Colorado territory. The development of additional wind then resulted in the spread of grass pollen. This coincided, not surprisingly, with the time frame of the heron's arrival. Similarly, the Herons' need for wind to fly, their hollow bones and dependence on the open space of the prairie are all grounds for what amounts to a high correlation of environmental dependence.

Also included in his writings was a short segment of a somewhat uncharacteristic style. Horatio penned the following passage, prefaced with the comment that it was neither meant to persuade nor dissuade, but may, in relationship to his research, offer a rather "interesting" insight in better understanding his studies.

> —I dreamed I was standing up to my knees in a river, and on either side of me were Great Blue Herons. We stood not speaking, watching the sun rise as though it were a song, a beautiful song of songs. Although all was silent. All was mute. I felt I could hear something, but the Herons, after watching the sun completely peak over the horizon, bobbed their heads a few times, straightened their necks and pointed their bills toward the sky. They lightly danced. I continued to stand still. This was the end of the dream and I wondered about a passage in the Bible, the Song of Solomon, not that this was that song, but perhaps it was a demonstration of love between me and the earth, or representative of the life between species, or better yet, between the land and the Herons. Maybe, just maybe, I had glimpsed into the nature of love.

In search of more valuable anecdotes on the Herons I began to retrace what I could of the work and life of Horatio Flatstone. This was not easy. His documentation was not only far reaching, but very idiosyncratic, eclectic and sparse. His little-read book I had chanced upon at the bookstore only included five obscure references, one of which I have not been able to verify. Another reference, however, was a strangely personal one which I was literally able to locate near the very rookery I was using for my study. Finally, there was one additional "non-academic" reference quoting some lines of poetry, by Baudelaire.*

Just as important as Horatio's writings have been several reproductions of his field drawings. There are also duplications of his handwritten field notes. These notes and drawings appear in the generous and well designed margins of the publication which appears to have been an effort to reproduce both Horatio's naturalist and journalistic attitudes alongside his stoic and ambitious scholarly research on the Great Blue Heron.

The field drawings range from quickly done abstractions of red tailed hawks and sycamore trees, to intricate and colored drawings of Heron nests. Interpreting his drawings, text, short notes and the other information I had already discovered through my own research, I became convinced of two vital details about the Great Blues:

1) I have come to know the very location of the tree from which the first Great Blues entered our world during that

---

*Clearly identifiable references cited in Horatio Flatstone's publication:

–"Ornithology and the Study of Alephs," R.A.S.'ta Lecuona, *Journal of Ornithology & Rune Stones* (©1912, vol. 32., no.8)

–*Herons: The Great Blue*, Crystal Karlye (D.A.L.&C. Gabaldon Productions & CDS Publishers Inc., Ltd +/- Esq'rd., ©1903, ff. 89)

–"Works of Celestial Creation in Collaboration with Form Line Art," article in *Cranes Across America*, Dakota y Spencer, et. al. (Ascension Press, Maddening, Indiana ©1876, 3rd printing, via lino-pressed oil paper)

–*Birds In Orthodox Russia*, The Hon. & Very Reverend Bishop Carreull Warrinnik (B Knorr Books, Munich Cycle Haus Q ©1899)

long night during the Miocene age so many million years ago.

2) I know the spot where the first fossilized remains of the Great Blue are known to be. The spot, I assume, along with Horatio, that the first Herons fly to in order to best extinguish themselves, following their initial birth from the tree mentioned above. A resting ground to echo their birthing ground.

Of these two facts the first is obviously perhaps more interesting. Yet it is by no means unimportant to know the location of this bird's prehistoric remains and what turns out to be its original, mid-North American continent habitat. Habitat is, to a large degree, responsible for a creature's habits (and vice versa). This knowledge has provided many stepping stones for me, even though the logic is somewhat circular in influence.

For the record, I should mention that the word "altar" was frequently included in the handwritten notes of Horatio. He seemed to believe that the nests, or at least the view of the nests, upward, from his position, offered a vestal shape.

Paul Shepherd may add to our understanding with a term, "parochial orbit," since the birds and their nests seem to suggest a microcosmic-like orbit of their own. The rookery as a whole, and the rounded nests themselves, are no doubt tended by some invisible and natural form of vestal virgin, be it the form of mist, clouds, magical energy, maybe even the beams of some shape of ever-reflecting sunlight.

After reading Dr. Flatstone's book several times, it was clear that the Heron was for Horatio as much a study of the history and phenomenon of angels as it was the study of ornithology. With wide outstretched wings, the Heron is on a journey amongst the entire spectrum of what are considered the nine realms of heaven. One of the reproductions in Horatio's book was the following passage: "I sense a tie between the angel and the Heron to have roosted in my head. These birds are as much in the air, of the air, perhaps they are air itself, at least relatives of wind."

A shared reference was also cultivated between Horatio and me. I learned that there was a local man named Fillmore Grin that was mentioned in Horatio's notes. I stumbled over this when I noticed there was an old mailbox near the route I took to the rookery with the name Grin on it. I admired the name in and of itself, but had no idea that Horatio and I were perhaps researching and examining the very same rookery of Blue Herons.

Horatio cited Fillmore Grin as, "an older gentleman who lived right nearby the rookery" and without the supposed advantages of academia, remained a man of "extraordinary understandings of natural history and regional lore." Horatio also stated, "I never considered Mr. Grin would hold up as a reliable source for my studious activities, but after a period of time I understood that he knew more than what was expected of the *academic*."

One evening I was told about a piece of writing Mr. Grin had created during the last years of his life. I was told that he had only spoke of this "writing" with his close friends and family. He had called his writing *The Wild Testament*. Being a rather tight-laced Missouri Synod Lutheran, Fillmore was always a bit nervous about telling anyone his real thoughts on the natural world. He told people in town and in his congregation he was a Lutheran through family tradition, but a naturalist by choice. If he'd been asked to choose between the two, he said he'd rather not have to and that it would be best to leave good enough alone.

I began to question the people in my Jefferson township about both Horatio Flatstone and Fillmore Grin. I looked through some old copies of newspapers and found nothing. Librarians seemed to know nothing, but the staff was mostly less than forty years old. I asked around at gas stations and grocery stores and from time to time someone remembered the names, or that the Grins had lived out of town a ways. Most of the pieces of information I discovered came during community fundraisers, such as an Optimists' pancake breakfast. In fact, it was a Veterans' pork chop dinner that led me to Mr. Flu Bats and sure enough, he had heard of them both. Flu was appropriately named, for his nose seemed to drip all the time and his sneezes were frequent and explosive. He was a retired hardware store owner. He didn't honestly think many knew of either Horatio, or Fillmore, but he had served them both at the store and each had revealed they were curious about birds, Herons in particular. In Flu's opinion, Horatio had picked up studying the Great Blue Heron's where Fillmore had left off. They had both been drawn to a slow, meandering creek near the Grin farm that runs through their place into tight valley for these parts of the country, along the Leavenworth and Jefferson county lines. Flu had been told by Fillmore, when he was buying some knife blades, tape and a pen about the scrap book Fillmore had begun to put together.

Over time Fillmore had confessed he was quite enamoured of the Herons and had started putting down some ideas on paper "about the world based on his observations of them."

"As far as I know," added Flu, "it was never read by anyone but Horatio, who had discovered it quite by accident. I imagine the book is still sitting out there somewhere."

"As far as I know, Horatio read it and put it back where he found it." Flu kind of smirked, "that Heron sure works the mind I guess, seems someone's always coming along wanting to know just a little bit more and more about them."

Flu told me he knew pretty much for certain that Fillmore's writings had been done by hand. He'd never seen the book by Horatio, he went on to say, "I didn't really expect he was taking it as seriously as he was. He seemed charmed by the birds, but I'd never have guessed he would have written anything." Flu added more, regarding Fillmore: "I expect most of his writing was done while under the influence of some pretty strong arthritis medicine he began having to take the last five years or so of his life."

In order to verify and discover the validity of Fillmore and Horatio's book, I began a relentless quest to actually locate the spot where the *Wild Testament* was in hiding. I followed the directions of Horatio's book and the clues from the area residents. I couldn't understand how anything bad could come of this.

In a stumbling manner of luck, I actually found the *Wild Testament*. Horatio had mentioned a hollow and large-trunked sycamore tree in his writing, and this tree had caught my attention time after time during my walks in to the rookery. The tree was right along the best trail. The tree had always seemed too large to me to be of no consequence to the region. I had often stopped and admired the girth of this huge, hollow trunk. I had an inkling that it was vital to the area, but never imagined its full importance. Yet it was this tree that contained the collection of writings Fillmore called his *Wild Testament.* There was more though. This tree was the very stem from which the Great Blue Heron had been born from during the Miocene so many years before. It was the center of the Heron's world, and perhaps this explains why this rookery keeps drawing the attention of curious naturalists like myself.

I have since read the document and returned it to its original location. There it rests, as you read this now, just as Mr. Grin placed it and where Horatio found, read and returned it. It truly felt like the birds and trees and wind were keeping a close watch on me while I read. For the record, I never removed the document from the forest. I read it in the woods where it was written and only took a few notes regarding the parts I found absolutely fascinating.

The esoteric volume was sparsely written, jumpy but firmly connected with the local environment. All references were to things visible within a couple hundred yards from where I sat, mention of the small creeks, seasonal plant varieties and such. There were no comparisons with places like California, or Europe. What set the book apart from other books was a strong reliance on common-sense and astute observation.

The book proved the importance of this particular place on the earth. The book was anything but boring. There were no rambling digressions. The handwriting was dark and the lead of the pencil and ink from pen had left imprints in the paper. The forms were labored, not flowing. The O's were more rectangular than circular. Mistakes weren't erased, but either written over or scribbled over to correct.

Any prior thoughts I had of Fillmore being in some way deranged, or of being a good-for-nothing eccentric, left my mind. Instead he became a genuinely good-natured, observant local hermit, engrossed in a close and intimate observation of the immediate world around him. He seemed in utter unison with the natural, spiritual, psychic, mystic, and meteorological, even with the colors and odors around him.

I marveled at the manner in which he had been able to stand back and observe the area which contained the Great Blue Heron rookery. Fillmore had obviously watched and studied the birds intently. He didn't comment on the Herons as a group, but had started a rather interesting and peculiar naming of the birds as though they were Angels, Saints, and Prophets. He assigned each creature a name and a piece of holy, *Wild Testament* scripture. I will include a few short examples below.

These bits of writing were like seeds, items that he had dreamed of. He seemed able to probe the very habits of rain drops which, like the Great Blues, returned each year—the rain to regenerate new life, the Herons to sit atop their thrones at the very back of the valley. He knew each element of the rookery was capable of speaking and even though he knew the Herons and the rain didn't return just for him, he pretended they did and worshipped the land because he knew if he cared for the land, then he was caring for the birds. If he were able to please the birds then they would tell him things and if he could just do everything right, then they would reveal magic and truth and comfort and grace. For each bird, each nest, each tree contained stories of the land. He felt the world in these birds as a liturgy. The following passages are excerpts from the *Wild Testament* which I found to be fascinating, make of them what you can:

†Via Saint Angus Dew (the one with the extra long plume feathers) Heaven must surely be made of memories, where the dearest details loom, then visit and return, recalled as clear as a song of the northern loon.

†Via Prophet Huett Longmaul, aka Sir Seth, (the one with the brightly colored beak): Listening doesn't mean waiting for your chance to speak.

†As told by Saintess Ah-Ha: The rain here is the rain of there. The sun here is the sun of there. The cry here is the cry of there. The cloud here is the cloud of there. The hopes here are the hopes of there. I know as anyone knows and know of what anyone will ever know. All of the time, I know I knowest and all of this is true.

†As said by Seraphim Rufus Splatter (while all six of his extraordinary wings did flutter). The prophet shall be of a different form and odor, neither camouflaged nor ashamed. Barred and in no way slippery. The prophet shall leave footprints which have no

replication; with a lingering scent of ash and bacon. Feet tipped with clear, rounded, white nails, but for the right, third digit, it shall be tipped with the color gold.

†Guardian Angel Azlea (she landed on her nest with a sense of balance not seen in any other) uttered and I repeat her words precisely, "Call this world a Wild Testament, Fillmore." She was influenced somewhat by her retired Southern Baptist mate, Thelbert D. Ogoleby. She believed, and reverently so that, "Religion is more about paying your bills on time than reciting the Lord's Prayer on Sunday. This, mixed with knowing the angle of the sun, makes all the difference in the world."

†Saint Emo sayeth perched from a sycamore branch—the wild comes straight in through the eye, and the eye is fully trained, not just in night vision, but in hypnotics too. Seeing as wind blows, knowing as pollen knows, just when and where each birth awaits arrival.

"Creation not only exists,
it also discharges truth."
—Gerhard Von Rad

3. Exploring Prehistoric

In every love affair there is a threat of the fantastic as well as
the potential for complete and devastating heartbreak. Such
is my interest with the Great Blue Heron. Placing my deepest
concerns with this creature has been wide and far reaching.
Having grasped a way into the heart of the natural world,
I've discovered that the Herons have brought ecstastic visions
and epiphanies of a surreal nature to me. Their simple, yet
complex, reptilian appearance has caused me to question my
sanity. Theodore Roszak suggests that questing to be amidst
other creatures is "where many might say sanity leaves off: at
the threshold of the nonhuman world." I have to admit I am
thirsty for this "insanity" though, am drooling in a maniacal
way for a glimpse of a world filled with Herons, especially if
that would make me ripe with crazy and enlightened forms
of magic and understanding. If only they could allow me
to tune into scents in the air, or able to hear silence, I'd be
the luckiest man alive. Yet, I am not expectant of a miracle.
I am slightly hopeful that the Herons may emit a pinch of
contagious magic over me which I could inhale, but I know
better. As Paul Gruchow says, "the only remark of nature is

its silence, but that is not because the world around us has nothing to say, it is because we come unequipped with ears to hear." I accept my limitations and take comfort in wonder.

I think nothing of seeing the grove of sycamore trees where these birds reside and aching with confusion, spinning in vertigo. I don't believe that a person can inhabit the realm of the rookery, the Herons, and the sycamores without reverie. Roszak adds that seeing the nonhuman world places us within "our most private spiritual travail." Dr. Flatstone, Fillmore Grin, and I are evidence of this, and we are not alone. Many people quest after different sorts of animal forms as well as plant and even fungi species in order to try and discover our ties to some long-ago, now forgotten language.

Our current version of modern human life has created a separation between mind and matter (not to mention that which matters), and it seems every day I hope that we are riding the crest of the heavenly spheres and that soon our language and actions and values will return to a sustainable, less consumptive state. Our Precambrian minds and genes will awake from their slumber and once again react to the subtle chirp of a bird. Our itching scalps will remind us that rain is on the way. There seems to me, as I walk in to see the Herons and am able to spot iris, mushrooms, and creek water moving, that our basic alchemy is disturbed—our above seems to be torn from our below. There is no way to underestimate the teachings of the mystics and their love of inspiration. Their belief that insightful flashes of knowledge and intuition could be tied to the workings of the color green, the light of sun, the glow of the moon, and for such a long and enduring period of time, is not to be taken lightly.

Birds have always been considered flashes of insight. Landscape painters, such as Hieronymous Bosch, have always wanted to depict the world as though they were birds. Auspicision, need we be reminded, is the bird presenting clues, answers, responses to our dreams. By walking to the top of hills and mountains to accentuate the *view* and by using grand and ephemeral *prospects* to present their interpretations, painters hope to present the world as angels, birds, or ghosts.

I feel like a child, or perhaps remember being a child, in the presence of the Great Blue Herons and once again feel the thrill of special outdoor places where I used to cuddle up in the fall weather as a ten-year-old, on a compost heap, along a limestone wall out of winter wind, warmed by the gentle sun. Or I would wander a path in the snow, following it to an opening in the woods to watch as the sun went down and the earth started to glow a dark and deep, metal ore-like color. I lived more in make-believe than in reality, but certainly not less in truth than I do now. My world was entirely true and imagined at the same time. All the world was candy, greened with sunlight, spiced with the gentle coos of the mourning dove. Remembering this now, I find myself recollecting a poem of e.e. cummings:

> i thank You God for most this amazing
> day: for the leaping greenly spirits of trees
> and a blue true dream of sky; and for everything
> which is natural which is infinite which is yes.

There is a starting point for all this reverie and belief around these Herons. Although mentioned earlier, it is worth repeating, that Dr. Flatstone makes mention of the tremendously wide trunked sycamore tree at the beginning of his journey to the Heron rookery. This hollow, goliath tree he states to be "the very hole through which the Herons emerged to create their brief constellation so many years ago." Aware that this sounds as likely as a hurricane in central Kansas, I will explain.

Peering into the darkened cavern of this gigantic sycamore I distinctly observe what appear to be the scrapes of claws and the coloring of feathers rubbed off on the trunk's inner surfaces. Following the angle of the tree's trunk, I can postulate the flight into space of the birds, and at night, with my eyes squinting, can predict where their light will emerge in a few million years, revealing the truth of this postulation. I shout down the hollow tunnel and it takes at least five or six minutes for an echo to return.

Just as it may have been for Horatio, this giant tree marks the beginning of my Great Blue journey since this tree is what first tickled my mind that something unique existed nearby. The tree seems to prophesy, in hermitic and mystic fashion, an understanding of the region. There are infinities of all sizes located around this tree. Thinking about the world is easy: everything around me tells a story of what it is like to live right here now and then and tomorrow. I reach back in my memory to recall the single point which contains everything. There is a story by Jorge Luis Borges entitled *The Aleph,* in which the aleph is explained in such a way as to make the dictionary useless. Borges says of the aleph, "the sum total of the spatial universe is to be found in a tiny sphere barely over an inch across." Recognition of this spot would come to a person instantaneously upon seeing it. Similarly, in an instant, I have chosen, for the joy and the agony which will come my way—the tips of the sycamore trees, their nests, flight and actions of the Great Blue Heron to be my mentors and spirit guides. I know this means all things will stretch in beautiful confusion with no end in sight. I consider how the world is full of an unlimited supply of holiness and this thought makes my momentary life seem inexplicable without a trust in the value of spirituality.

On a journey, then, past this hermitic tree, I follow the direction of the creek beside me, gazing upward and forward in anticipation of the rookery. It is purely amazing how well the birds blend their long necks, their arching flight and spectacular nests into their surroundings. It is not long before I spot a few of the birds in flight, landing, flying, barking, squawking, frahhwking in spring busyness. My heart churns like a geyser. I take a deep breath and prepare to enter the Heron's sacred ground.

As I get nearer and nearer, I finally feel no more than the whiff of a whisper, the lightest puff of the letter "Y" in my emptied mind. I bow, sit down, watch, listen, and contemplate with all my senses wrapped together. Peeking up the first time, I feel slightly invasive, as though spying on someone who would be offended at my peering, and I notice one of the Great Blues, perched on the inner cup of a nest, sitting still amongst the flights and flurry of other Herons, peering directly at me. The bird does not move or twitch or seem self conscious. It only keeps staring into my eyes. We look at each other, and it seems as though we are communicating with our hearts not our minds, our ears, our mouths—both of us, I imagine, wondering what the other is. After a span of maybe twenty minutes, this single Great Blue utters a high pitched whistle. An approval of some sort? I am not certain. However, what does become clear is that there is a reversal of my intention on this journey, which has taken me by surprise. I feel immersed in warm soft water: I have become the observed. I have heard that to observe nature is as though being part of scripture, so what does it mean to become the observed? I reason this is why Dr. Flatstone included the small portion from the poet Baudelaire:

> We walk through the forests of physical things
> that are also spiritual things
> that look on us with affectionate looks (7:44)

*"Curiosity cannot receive a genuine response
to what it investigates if the person cannot
tolerate emotional disturbance."*
—Shierry Weber Nicholsen

4. The Flavor of Brass

Discovery of the Great Blue Heron nests is not possible without careful attention. These creatures of the air inhabit silent spots at the back of wilderness, where creeks slide each moment through stands of phosphoric and glowing, flaking and chipping sycamore trees.

The Heron is a wild creature and a majestic recluse who refuses to reside where other creatures, especially humans, or another of its major antagonists, the bald eagle, will find it. The Herons' nests are intended to be secrets. Looking for them is a guessing game.

I have been lucky to observe Herons near enough to hear them breathing. Their gaze is something akin to pure emotion—not so much sadness, glee, or impatience, but a smooth and curling weave of morning fog, twisting skyward, joining thin veiled cumulus clouds. The Heron's yellow-edged eyes raise the hairs on my arms and neck and prick goose bumps on my arms. The stare of this bird is not so much *at* me, as *into* me. I imagine it thinks my lungs would taste exceptional, as easy to scoop from me as a tadpole out of the Kaw River.

When the Heron moves its gaze off me and lifts one foot gently out of the water, forward, without rippling the shallow water it is standing in, it makes as much noise as grass seed growing, the sound of an ant sneezing. I continue to stare, and no thoughts enter my mind. I am fixated on the Heron's every move and feather. A duck flies in from overhead and breaks my trance. At the same instant, the Heron flails and flaps away. My imagination runs rampantly—are these birds long-ago dwarfs with wings? I reach the same conclusion: the Heron seems to be living in a different time and place from me. I wonder to myself: *is the blue Heron in search of solitude, or is the blue Heron trying to find its way out of solitude?* They resemble ancient and austere hermits on a secret, mystical journey while dwelling at the center of the world.

The Great Blue Heron possesses a pair of wings big enough to shadow an entire valley. When spooked off the branches of a high rising sycamore tree, they let loose guttural belches— grumbly, bedrock laden "frrhawks" sounding more like roots than the mere movement of feathers and air.

Long tendril-legs place this bird as much as four-and-a-half-feet off the ground. These slender legs allow the bird to miss the ruffle of wind, while providing a vehicle to move without ripple through high water. Often considered a coarse creature with leathery legs and feet, the Heron also displays a commit-ted sense of honor and delicacy. For instance, the male Heron finalizes its marriage each spring by offering the female a twig to add to the nest.

In moments of prenuptial bliss, the Heron will fly three or four minutes, in a giant circle, four to five hundred yards wide, with neck outstretched, circling in the hemisphere as though creating a wedding band in the sky. An adept creature of the Middle West, a Heron needs vast and isolated air space to live, only feeling at home in areas such as Northeast Kansas, with its wide-open landscape and little-known tree-filled valleys.

The Great Blue is a primeval species. It reminds people of some sort of reptile. The shape of its head and neck, together with lightly crimson legs, make it appear somewhat as the tongue of a lizard.

Perched in a silent, isolated world amongst the bloom of woodland flowers, the birds hide nothing. They boldly displays primal instincts—tapping, snapping, touching, and bowing their bills with one another. The male clasps the neck of the female with his long orangish bill while mating. This is definitely not a position to take lightly. The bill of the Heron is a dangerously sharp weapon, serrated along the edges, and can be catapulted forward with the energy contained in its eighteen-to-twenty-inch neck—a neck fully spring-loaded with a network of ferocious muscles. It is no problem at all for a Heron to puncture the skull of a man or woman.

The bird is easily insulted by intrusion. When I spot a Heron along a river while canoeing or on my way into the rookery, I notice there is no hesitation in the way the bird churns out a large gobbet of runny white guano as its long legs trail and wide wings fiercely flap. In a light wind, I often pick up the slightest whiff of the Heron's breath, revealing an odor I can best describe as that of green moss on the shady side of tree bark, a sanctuous aroma additionally spiced with the pungency of worm casings and piles of dew-soaked cedar shavings.

Beneath a Heron's nest fall the bones of the unsuccessful. In survival of the fittest fashion, the newborns begin battle early in life for pieces of regurgitated food offered by their parents. In these fights of subsistence, often siblings push brother or sister from the highest tips of the tall trees, thus creating compost for the sycamore trees towering above. This is a rude lesson in sympathetic magic—the herons sacrificing themselves for their local environment, thanking the trees and creek for their role in their ultimate survival.

My admiration for the Great Blue is as intense as its evolution has been. I believe that if I were offered a cup of a Heron blood to drink, I would do so without hesitation. I am most alive when I am in their presence. The intimacy I feel with these birds suggests I am involved in a form of initiation. I am transported through the divisions between cultured humanity and nature's wildness. Instead of needing money and worrying about how my neighbor mows his lawn, I am engrossed in the basest ingredients of the greedy, full-blooded harmony of the natural world. My body and mind go plunging into the workings of the clouds and wind, to observe the tips of the Heron's wings, whose ends bend and fall with the air when flying. Each time I visit the rookery, I feel these things inside me. I close my eyes and see fire and water, earth and air, and I sense a holy spirit. I become enveloped in awe and get carried away to where time goes much too slowly to even exist. I am transposed to where deep, long ago stories of the land reside. To that wild place where poet W.S. Merwin suggests resides the realm of our "forgotten language."

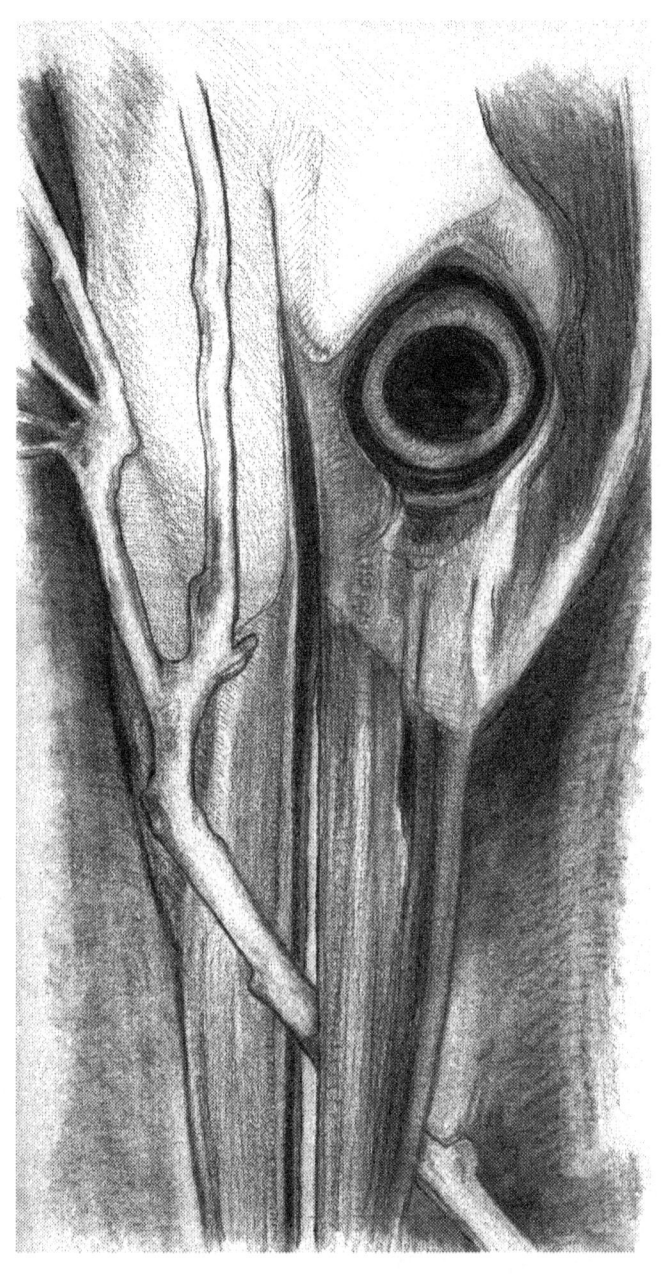

Standing beneath the Heron's nest, stooping over and picking up one of the infant's bones, my armpits begin to drip, and my lips become dry. I rummage through my mind, raise my eyebrows, and hear a line of William Faulkner echo around inside my ears: "A flavor like brass in the sudden run of his saliva, a hard sharp constriction either in his brain or his stomach, he could not tell which and it didn't matter." As though these words were a prayer, I go over them again and again, knowing this rookery is a sacred spot. My hands and fingers constrict with the thought. This place is love and instinct made of first-born thoughts. Even as I experience this place, I begin to long for it to continue.

This prehistoric world of the Great Blue provides one last vision. A Great Blue walks up beside me, and we meditate on the flow of water. The earth stalls, and I spot frogs moving between beams of sunlight in the water. I see in the reflections of the creek water that the Great Blue is cloaked in a robe of gray and blue, preened and covered with waterproof dust, gleaming with a robust and shiny sheen in the evening sunshine. Such Herons are prophets of the prehistoric—disguised with wings and feathers. Moving out of my trance, I hear feathered wings flap hard, and although I look quickly for the bird, even try to spot a moving shadow, I see nothing.

Ecologist and philosopher David Abram has said, "To listen to the forest is also, primordially, to feel oneself listened to by the forest." And so I stand, looking and wondering if the Great Blue can hear what I hear. Can the Heron hear my heart beating loudly?

*"Magic, then, in its primordial sense, is the
experience of existing in a world made
up of multiple intelligences."*
—David Abram

5. Nests and Extremity

On average, the clutch of eggs laid by the Great Blue Heron is four. While one of the bigger species of birds, the size of the great blue's egg is smaller than might be expected. Given that this species of Heron stands much taller than the screech owl, a ten-inch bird, it seems strange that the screech owl's egg is actually larger. In the alchemical world, this detail is not insignificant. The Great Blue Heron's egg must necessarily contain a highly concentrated life force, maybe inside the egg shell rests a potion comprised of helium, which manifests upon birth, so that, when the small baby Heron makes contact with the air surrounding the rookery, an expansion occurs unlike that of the screech owl.

It is likely the Great Blue goes through two stages of imprinting. The baby Heron's first imprint is with their parents. The second imprint starts soon thereafter, as soon as their eyes can clearly discern depth-of-field. This imprint is with the long angular branches of the sycamore tree, the smell of creek water filtered across limestone, and the sounds of earthworms digging in the rich soil beneath the Heron nests. If you try to distinguish the shape of the grown Heron's neck and legs from the branches of a sycamore tree, it becomes clear that the two are remarkably similar.

The Great Blue's eggshell is a careful blending of pale blue with the slightest slightest tint of green. This coloring allows the egg to merge with their habitat: the large bird's piece-mealed, scattered, palimpested platform nests among the trunks of the sycamore trees. This evolutionary coloring of the egg is an act of pure genius I like to fantasize. I imagine that the slightest coloring of the eggs may cause a crow to pause just long enough, confused as to whether the eggs are leaves, a twig, or a chunk of sycamore bark, and thus keep the unborn Heron from becoming just a bite to eat, until a parent can quickly return. In reality, I'm told, it rarely works this way. The Crows and Eagles aren't confused.

ii.

Sir James George Fraser, author of *The Golden Bough*, stated that "ancient people, prehistoric animals, even plants, have been able to place their souls outside themselves as a method of protection, maybe even as a way to rest the body and the soul."

There is something startling and intriguing about this idea of a soul external and the ability to place a soul outside the self somewhere in the wider world. This act sounds at the very same instant both remarkably possible and yet dauntingly impossible.

Could any of us be so lucky as to place our souls off to the side and let them rest unattended? Could we set aside our

soul and let it soak in the moon's gentle creamy light, or allow our soul (or spirit we might even say) to be enriched inside a fox den, or secured and swirling in an eddy of cool spring creek water? Such thoughts seem almost too luxurious, but certainly worth wishing for.

When I think of the amount of misdirected momentum that our "modern" life has created, I know that something as intricate, delicate, and precise as placing a soul externally would involve far too much patience to be accomplished by a human being. Nine-and-a-half out of ten of us are far too concerned about paying mortgages or wondering about the next special at the super-duper mainstream quadraspectacular-mart-o-rama. A soul is unique and needs to be in balance—not embraced by just one sudden moment, but with thought and care, using a process of ritual. This is not how we are inclined to live. There is a lack of self-sufficiency and, as a result, a loss of personal empowerment. Northeast Iowa writer Robert Wolf sums our predicament up well: "[People] are no longer able to see things as aspects of Infinity, but see all things as finite and measurable." Placing the soul requires that we make the commitment of our life, which is perhaps as infinite a commitment as we can make. The soul of the Heron is outdoors and hiding and living comfortably with infinity. Their options are wind and rain, sun and stone. Dirt or leaves. Their world is not one of red lights, due dates, warranties, or dial tones. What comes their way is not nearly as important as being able to survive what comes their way. Perhaps their days are slower than ours, not broken down in seconds and minutes but in sunlight to sunset. Summer to fall. Their migrations are based on the angle of the sun, but in no way are their lives less complex.

Somewhere in my ancient, latent mind I know placing the soul externally is all-important. I crave the compassion and insight required to integrate a soul to the burl of an oak tree, and the spiritual and invisible acts required. I know the idea rests in me somewhere since the very notion of placing a soul is a conundrum that sounds so right yet at the very same moment impossible. Taoists suggest, "The way is easy, strive hard." Placing the soul externally is not difficult. Just figure out how and where.

If any living thing could place a soul externally, it would be the Great Blue, this sleek and persistent prophet of the prehistoric. Yet the Great Blue is not a normal prophet. They are prophets of the extreme, and in their presence we are awestruck, timeless, and remain speechless. Historian of thought Allan Megill points out that, "The prophets of extremity put up a distorting mirror against our world." The Great Blues, without trying (to continue quoting Megill), "help us break out from a deadening routine, from the petrification." When the Herons fly away, after a quick glimpse of their movement, we agonize and question their natural existence as if we know that somewhere in our deep pulse we once knew the songs of richly sedimented sand-bars and the walk of the Heron as well as we now read an issue of the daily newspaper. American philosopher William Hocking said, "The prophet is the mystic in action." I truly believe this to be the case of the Great Blue. As well, in the words of Matthew Fox, "The mystic in every one of us trusts his or her experience of the divine in nature, which opens our hearts...the trust of our experience is the basis of all mysticism."

Longevity is needed in order to place, revisit, and refresh the soul external, which is exactly the point. For eons, humans were in close communication with the whole variety of life on earth, not just with themselves and their self-created systems and techniques. The Great Blues, by nesting in the same spots year after year, are involving themselves in ritual, which evokes a power of place and proves (rather than records) importance.

Placing a soul externally requires an uncommon ability to be cloaked in secrecy. A Blue Heron's rookery is a wonderful spot, since they nest and mate and raise their young only when they have reason to believe they will be amidst complete privacy. Not only this, but it can't be just a passing detail that the Herons have picked the sycamore tree, both the largest and oldest tree of the Midwest in which to reside. Beyond this, the oldest remains, as mentioned by Horatio Flatstone, of the Great Blues rest on the vast open space of the Great Plains in Nebraska, a day's flight perhaps, north of this rookery and the birth place of the Heron.

At first it is not necessary to associate the Great Blue Heron with the sycamore tree; it just happens that both I and Dr. Flatstone have. The interesting correlation between the two can best be examined by theories of a soul external. As mentioned, the soul external is a magical placement, properly understood in the context of perception and longevity. The sycamore tree can play host to both of these needs since it is the longest living deciduous tree species in the Midwestern region, living on average three hundred years. During this time, a *siege* of Herons can certainly invoke the time needed to attend to any special needs that the soul external may require. Transferring, for example, the soul from one spot to another, from one to limb to the next as it evolves. The tree, like the Heron, is able to stand as a native to one particular spot. Is able to feed off of what a particular spot has to offer. Satisfied with the rain that comes during the year; satisfied with what sunshine comes its way, neither hoping for more, nor wishing for less. Living from what actually happens. Letting these years seep and create and develop allows for a soul as unique as the flavor of wild cherries from one place in a woodland to the next.

As for the oldest remains of the Great Blue Heron, that they are to be found in the earth of the Great Plains could be considered a coincidence, but it is doubtful. This makes perfect sense for a host of good reasons. The Midwest is hardly even thought of as any place by most of the people of the world, yet it is a coveted fly zone for birds and butterflies.

The precise location of the early remains are located at the Observation Quarry and indicate this early genus type is at least fourteen million years old. Think how many migratory flights have gone on beneath the watch and wings of the Great Blue then consider how many times a sycamore tree has been used as a nest. The vast open plains are sometimes referred to as the forgotten coast, or in older maps of the United States as the Great American Desert. My suspicion is that the Heron loves this sort of thinking. If the Herons were able to discern statistics and find out that population totals were declining in Kansas or Nebraska, they would probably add an extra congratulatory belch to their array of noises. Of course, where better to create a constellation for yourself? Blowing out of the ground amidst nothing but the solace of sky above. In a land that is known for being forgotten, lost and cast away.

Another advantage to residing on the Great Plains is the mating flight of the Great Blue, performed with its neck stretched out, which is not an easy maneuver for the bird. The Plains, however, provide ample space for this wide and peculiar action. Just as the body is 75-80% water, so the Great Plains are 75-80% sky and open space. Opportunities for all sorts of ways of flight are largely accessible. A vast, three-to-four-hundred-yard circular flight to impress a female even sounds somewhat Midwestern. It's not exactly a great pick-up line, or a verbal masterpiece, but it is a strong action that speaks for itself and impresses.

If you do come upon a rookery in a stand of sycamore trees somewhere in Kansas, Iowa, or Nebraska, stop all forward motion, stand still, do not move your neck, just twist your head, and eyes to look around. Spy for small altars hidden in the top branches. I agree with Dr. Flatstone on this: "that a rookery seems tended by a chorus of vestal virgins." There is a purity, an innocence and a beauty that expel air, that will mystify speech and thought. This I account for because of the presence of the soul external. Enter reverie, which is an emotion we feel when words go away.

iii.

Having visited the abandoned remains of Heron rookeries, I can attest that these spots seem hauntingly void of any external souls. Evacuated rookeries are clearly cheated of a sensible inheritance of continuous life. They lack a partnership with mystery and tradition. They are echoes and memories without beat, void of flapping, ominous realms of the sort that once harbored a sensuous and slowly evolving soul external. The partnership between spirit and soul has been removed, and the cause most normally comes from invasions of human noise or is a result of the soul external's discovery. The magic of the hidden soul, once discovered, goes away. This is a point made quite clear by Sir George Fraser in his *Golden Bough*. Pointing out a couple old stories, from regions such as Cambodia and Russia, will help sum up the state of the rookery once the soul external is discovered by the wrong creature. A daughter may ask, "Papa, where is your soul?" Fraser writes:

> Sixteen miles from this place, he said, is a tree. Round
> the tree are tigers, and bears, and scorpions, and snakes;
> on the top of [the] tree is a very great fat snake; on his
> head is a little cage; in the cage is a bird; and my soul is
> in that bird. (776).

When this bird is found and destroyed, so is destroyed the Papa. One frequently finds the soul external hidden in trees. Another example is:

> My death, said he, is far from here and hard to find, on
> the wide ocean. In that sea is an island, and on the island
> there grows a green oak, and beneath the oak is an iron
> chest, and in the chest is a small basket and in the basket

is a hare, and in the hare is a duck, and in the duck is an egg; and he who finds the egg and breaks it, kills me at the same time (778).

Unfortunately, someone does find the egg and does kill this man's soul and causes his death.

What is fascinating is the tie between the placement of the soul in trees with life. Through mystic intuition, perhaps, I know without any doubt this Heron rookery in Kansas harbors a soul external. The place is a sanctuary for deep, long-lasting and harmonious life. It is my opinion that it is the very soul of the species *Ardea herodias*, or rather the Great Blue Heron. This place offers clues as to the Heron's soul: there are the crowns and limber shapes of the sycamore tree, the winding, calming trickle of creek water, filtered through the top soil and humus of the sycamore's leaves, the remains and offerings of the Herons themselves. There is the blessing of the soft and continual breeze rattling tree tops and the gift of Cottonwood cotton. In this spot, beneath these nests, amongst the bones strewn on the ground, or inside the trunk of a tree, there *is* the hum and churning of a private, vital soul external in possession of the scent of the earthly elements, an odor distinctive yet indescribable. I will not, dare not, look for the soul external, though.

I believe I have been offered a secret. In order to give thanks, I need to protect and avoid being too specific about where this spot is. Somehow, I must share the soul external, but at the same time I must not give the soul away, since this will cause death. There is a level of trust that goes with knowing the soul's location. That the external soul can be placed in animals, inanimate objects, as well as trees, is at the same time helpful and that much more confusing. Does the Heron fly with the soul, and is it able to tend it in other places? Or does the Great Blue come to these particular spots for a period of time, checking on the soul's condition in the deep roots of the sycamore trees? It seems obvious that the Herons must nest and give birth somewhere hidden, and this could easily be in order to avoid being tempted by outsiders who may question where the soul they are caring for has been left.

Yet this whole soul external issue is even more fascinating. Fraser also explains the power of sympathetic magic. This magic is such that the one whom the soul belongs to never needs to retrieve it. Thus, in theory, one could hide a tangible soul in the mist and love of a sacred spot and then travel within the world's most hideous spots, but at no point would the person lose touch with beauty unless someone else were to discover and ruin their hidden soul. The soul resting in its secret, sacred spot is safely tended to and cared for. The comparison to the vestal virgins, tending reverently a fire for eternity, becomes appropriate in this regard, as one can rely on the eternity of the soul's safety.

The depth of the Great Blue's soul external is a miracle. They know of the oceans which once covered this realm of Great Plains. They are not ignorant that this vast landscape once housed peaks of a high reaching mountain range known as the Nemahas. The soul external of the Great Blue can recall without hesitation the wild stampede of the Bison. Not a single oceanic high tide, thunder bolt, or drip of glacier ice has been lost to the *Ardea herodias'* soul external. Their soul absorbs, churns, contains this landscape and all it has been.

It all seems too fantastic somehow. If it were not that I know the Great Blue to be a prophet, then I would doubt the pure depth of this experience. I mean, after all, what is a prophet (according to T.J.J. Altizer) but "one who speaks what is unsayable to others, but once spoken, immediately carries its own authority?" In spite of what I can observe and understand of the Great Blue in its fishing habits, styles of flight, nest creation, mating dances, beak tapping and migration patterns, it still remains an unknowable species to me. However, I know that I must listen, watch, and learn all the same, for there is never a time when the Great Blue is not living out the ways and methods of the wild and prehistoric.

In synch with my thoughts of prophets and Herons, I raise my eyesight to the highest tips of the stand of sycamore trees along the trail from the hermitic tree. I recognize the sounds of the downy woodpeckers in the background. I hear a red tail hawk squeal up high in the distance. I notice the light footwork of chickadees and peeps of the nuthatch. Concentrating on hearing the wind overhead, I imagine the depth and placement of the souls external being roosted and tended in this place, where the siege of Great Blues descend each year, here, on the Great Plains of eastern Kansas, in this remote corner of Jefferson County, along a creek that shall remain unnamed.

I look up to see forty, maybe fifty, even sixty nests globbed together like beaver dams, defying gravity, stick by stick perched and balanced into broad platforms which from below appear rounded as though planets. These nests are built upon year after year, until the wind blows them down, or they simply become so heavy the limb bursts off. How a family of large lanky birds can reside so high in the limbs of tree makes me delirious with wonder.

As though full moons, I see that the nests above me are glowing, humming, churning together the earthly elements of this place: bits of bark, twigs, mud, items from the air and water all palimpsested together. There is no greater thrill than to see these nests at dawn; or at dusk, the Herons returning; or leaving as though shooting stars, or angels in search of sunlight-enriched food.

I am reminded of the vestal virgins tending the Vestal fire, those pure hearted souls, attendant for the sake of sacred eternity. I actually believe that there can not be much difference between a soul external and a soul eternal. I know that the external soul is placed in order for rest, protection and the inheritance of knowledge. I have come to realize that what I call the wild, a Heron knows as everyday "normal."

iv.

The nests radiate an energy. My heart drops, pulling my breath down to my knees. I am undergoing a change. Is wandering amidst the souls of the Herons a sacred journey? It is as mysterious a thing as if I were to wake floating with cumulus clouds one morning.

It doesn't really matter how long these souls have been harbored in this grove of trees, or even how the separation of body, memory and the soul occurs. The variety of possibilities is so dense and timeless, my brain might as well be wandering an ancient labyrinth. I consider these souls to be holy objects, amulets from times even prior to the Miocene. I lightly whisper to myself, "Ashes to ashes…dust to dust." I am not sure why, except that I feel something here that once was nothing, born from out of mystic sensitivity. Of importance to me is to offer prayer to the Heron's soul, to touch the sycamore's trunk and drink the water moving elements through. (See five Heron prayers at end of book).

Using intuition, simply sitting in one place and looking up, I reflect on my life. It occurs to me that I have laid my eyes on a soul external before. Out of the corner of my eye, lying on a heap of leaves in my wooded childhood valley in Iowa, a chilled October morning, hours before my friends would get up, I heard three doves cooing nearby. Lazily, I gazed into this nowhere, but what I discovered instead of doves was a cluster of bright butterflies floating around my head, and instead of waving them away, I felt calm and watched their fluttering shapes wisp and rise and scatter as I tried to focus. The butterflies were not as real as the colors on their wings: incredible blurs of brightly tinted mushy liquid—blue-gold, green-silver, red-copper, yellow-brass, stars flashing tin. I felt amazed back then, nothing short of fascination and bewilderment. This became a secret held so tightly I'd forgotten it entirely, but now I wanted this moment back. Thomas Moore wrote: "A spiritual sensibility rises directly out the human encounter with the natural world." I had been offered a glimpse into a soul external when younger by the natural world.

Recovering childhood glory is the journey of the hero. I certainly feel heroic once again as I stand admiring the Great Blues, just as I did so many years ago when watching what may have, may not have been, the water-colored clump of butterflies. Remembering my childhood encounter with the soul external, it occurs to me that I am living a straight, yet forever curving path up toward the wide open sky above me. Always, ever so slightly, ever so constantly I am in one way or another preparing for flight.

I am clinging as narrowly as a cliff swallow's nest to the edges of certainty as I explore the meanings and location of this thing called the soul external. If such a thing is as true as I believe, then it is an ancient practice which has been going on millions and millions of years. Perhaps because I need to have certainty, faith, grace in my life, I cling to this theory as anyone does who wishes for the eternal. I know this has its possible drawbacks. What any of us anywhere know is only as certain as a story, a wish, or magic. Even theology, writes William Gass, "appears to be one half fiction, one half literary criticism."

I suppose, then, I am one half understanding this great rookery and the soul external to be real, but I am one half wondering if I am not making things up, wishing for what I want in spite of contrary, even non-existent evidence. However, I do not understand this to be a problem, for I agree, conveniently or not, with Señor Jorge Luis Borges, who professed from the library of his mind that, "My story will be true to reality, or in any case, my personal memory of reality, which amounts to the same thing."

As I gather this sense of certainty and joy, I seem to become almost as quickly full of sorrow. I'm not satisfied with theory, with philosophy, and I feel cheated, because I want to sense more intimacy with the beauty of the sycamore trees and the slabs of bedrock lining the creek. I would like to be closer to the loose sticks lying on the ground, those lucky strands of wood which become parts of the Heron's nests.

I take comfort that once humankind did battle to know the world like a snake or the tangles of wild rose vines. Partly inspired by beauty and partly inspired by intuition, I have wished to be swayed in the realm of this rookery by the mystic Hildegard of Bingen, who understood that a place such as this could exist in a soulful way, known through instinct and intuition, generating power from the color and life of the color green.

The Heron is a prophet in the manner which Hildegard suggests, since the space where it resides is able to "illuminate the darkness." That is to say, each time I visit this spot I am brought out of myself and into a new, "universe with a different quality, an entirely different world, transcendent and holy." It may seem overly sentimental to suggest that I have seen the light, or found a holy spirit, yet each exploration into the space of the Great Blue does bring me closer to the creativity of the world and how I and the species fit together. Each visit brings me closer and closer to understanding the difference between solitude and silence. I realize that watching these large ancient creatures making noises in the woods is, although loud, absolutely silent at the same time. They are similar to wind overhead in the leaves of Cottonwoods, or of the noise waves bring after they are created from the silence of the sea. I have become mesmerized into a state of solitude.

Contemporary writer Kathleen Norris states that mystic sensibility is able to, "see, hear and know simultaneously." Precisely. In the "viriditas" way of being, there may exist the work of an indefinable God: a deep and unfathomable force of consistency based upon continual, creative renewal that I believe comes to roost through mystic sensibility. This is what may be contained in the soul external, who knows? I am satisfied with the bold and brilliant colors of my childhood and the slow glow of faith being born in me with each visit to the rookery. I wish for the greening power to tend me, care for me, keep me growing, full of hope and sprouting.

Understanding the realms of any place is limitless. This rookery is no exception. There is no end to understanding. More brings more, less brings more. Nothing is immense. Immensity is overwhelming, and yet at times still not enough. A hermit is not a hermit entirely, but venturing in and away from time rather than out and with time.

This rookery is a wild journey, and fortunately I do not feel the need to travel far. In this sense of place rests a speck of all things. I am reminded of a story about an old lady from the Fourth Century. This lady revealed a lesson during a visit from St. Sarapion of Sinodite. It turned out that the woman had not moved, not even spoken or blinked her eyes, for decades, and as a result had become widely celebrated as a great recluse within the city of Rome. St. Sarapion, a well-respected wanderer, went to this lady and wondered, whispering in her ear, "My lady, you do not move? Why are you just sitting?"

To which the old lady slowly, quietly, replied, "Sir, do you not see? I am not sitting here, I am on a journey."

St. Sarapion must surely have felt confused. How could a single lady just sitting in place be on a journey. Was she not harboring a soul external? If it did occur to St. Sarapion, it must have occurred to him like a revelation that this lady was in fact on a journey.

What she was doing was developing a native Tao. The location of the Great Blue in Viriditas, Kansas, is just this, a teacher of instinct and intuition. I remind myself that these nests, these trees, the souls external are not just sitting here: they are on a journey. It is clear, now is the time to investigate the realm of the prophet of the prehistoric.

To investigate I suggest staying where you are. Dawns will come to you without any effort whatsoever. Gather twigs and build a nest in which to place your soul. Find solitude and then go in to the wild with your heart content. Try to find forgotten languages from whence we were able to let loose magic off our fingertips or through our eye balls. Remember when the earth was ash and dust and the wind blew and things happened without laws, rules, thought, or reason. Keep in mind that the strange is not incorrect, weird is not unusual, funky is not negative and that "the imaginal is intermediate between material and the spiritual." (Shierry Weber, 103).

5. Hermits and Madness

Perhaps because he passed away so young, but with such talent, the poet Keats is able to capture the surprises and wonders of the world. I quote him in relationship to the rookery: "Negative Capability is when a man is capable of being in uncertainties, mysteries, doubts, without any irritable reaching after facts and reason." What better way to describe the presence of the rookery and its environment. I accept this spot not as a well-groomed location comfortably laid out for the Heron, not as a pasture grazed by cattle, not as a perfect garden thoughtfully planned out to be just as mankind wishes, but as a spot that without courage I would wander into and cut and tangle and draw blood from myself in confusion. The realm of the Heron's birthing ground is wild as wild can be.

I come here with a faith of the natural world in my head, not one that congratulates myself as though I were alive and well atop the heap of some evolutionary pyramid, but one that rejoices in this sacred spot precisely because I know I become in-line with birds, moles, stream water, even microscopic protozoa.

There is a madness to this of course. A madness of originality and of the type shared by the hermit. I am at one with the "mad" man who creates, not the mad man who kicks and pounds the world with anger. It is only by considering there to be magic here, and in the spirit of magic I crave the sympathetic, contagious magic of the spirit world. The beauty of magic is such that it is not so unreal as we think. In many ways it is in opposition to spirit. One way of seeing magic is that it is a process of cause and effect, not at all dependent on blindness. I would be a fool to declare that I think magic is the sole explanation for the natural world and the charms of the Heron. I would be equally as foolish to declare that blind faith brings me all I need in relationship to the structure, beauty and mystic links the thrones of the Herons offer me.

If we are to take the mystic, alchemical imagery further we must suppose the equality of the below and the above. We must be willing to delve deep and high. William Occam proposed the ever-famous Occam's Razor theory to us which goes along these lines: "what we know is built upon emptiness, upon concepts and therefore one can stride straight to the source through intuitive cognition (*Notitia Intuitiva*)." How is this of any value? If we use our intuition we can travel straight to the Heron's side and my intuition allows me to find them to be angels.

What to make of the reverent bird in this light? The heron becomes a magical form, an angel with two large wings, is it a guardian of the natural world and a disciple of Saint Francis and all his followers. We present these hopeful and beautiful images of the Heron just as previous humans have presented all beautiful angels. As angel writer Malcolm Godwin concludes his book *Angels*, "If you really want to see an angel don't look for one outside: they reside within, and so long as human beings seek their own totality and wholeness, the angelic species cannot be endangered." This is definitely a useful way to see the Herons.

If I am to tell another person, as Horatio Flatstone and Fillmore Grin did, of the miracles of this rookery, I already know I will be shunned and met with responses of laughter and disbelief. Revealing ideas which can't be fully quantified or explained through standard spiritual doctrine (not to mention in a scientific manner) is nearly impossible, even if proven.

Take the account of St. Joseph of Copertino during the 17th century. The story starts without Joseph being a Saint, but merely an odd person and most likely a laughable one at that. After all, Joseph claimed he was able to fly. Not just like a high jumper, but that he could really really fly and float and move about in the ether of air. One day he went away from other people, to an obscure corner of the chapel where he was engrossed in prayer by himself. Suddenly he cried out: he had risen up in the air and was flying to a nearby altar. With another cry, he flew back to the corner where he had started his prayers. Joseph was investigated by the Church, acquitted of the charge of practicing deception of false miracles. Against the odds, Joseph was soon to become a Saint through the accounts and witnesses of "respectable" people. Actual observation finally proved he was able to fly. This one example is good proof of the impossible. Not easy to do, but the Catholic Church canonizes only those whom it conclude, beyond doubt, are capable of the acts claimed. I present this not so much as a testament to the power of a "God" but rather to make clear the possibilities that exist in this layered mindful world of ours.

Recently, a false complexity of our thoughts has occurred. Our inner layers of the brain have been taken captive by our thin and recent outer, momentary shells. We have started to believe that computers and cable television, as prime examples, are "necessities." Learning to understand the Heron (or more precisely, re-learning) requires probing way into the heart of the inner core of the mind. Into that one which craved shelter from the wind.

Staring straight ahead. Looking, not seeing. Gazing and not purposefully thinking. Weary of the shape of the clouds and the smell of the wind, I see the Heron foraging along the banks of the Kaw River. After so much time spent observing these birds over the past years I realize that seeing the Heron standing, waiting for food is really not an accurate indication of the Heron in a rookery. The variety of noise, the clamor and madness which ensues during the straightening of the nests, the mating and the feeding of the young is something which is hard to describe when most view the bird as solitary. To fully understand the heron it must be seen as part of a spot on earth. The bird is part of the sycamore tree, part of the water flowing in the creek, for it is partly the color green filtering throughout the valley, part plant roots and even partly the squeal of the hawks way overhead. The collection of all these things can be understood only as a sacred spot finally realized as the rookery and the Great Blues. It is within this realm that the soul external is harbored. There has never been a spot more ripe with the alchemy of place.

Can we learn to worship a creature supported by two thin legs and reaching as much as four and a half feet tall? Creatures that have evolved little since the Miocene era? Do we dare ignore the creative mythology of previous generations and the feeling of being healed through fear? Can we really be happy without being able to run amuck, ambushing our need for surprise? Pure reason is not really all that satisfying. This is why we put up with pesky pets, why we like rainstorms, why my favorite days are cold, windy and void of sun. I find primordial, deeply hidden and unusual instincts necessary to be satisfied.

Learning to speak silence is time consuming. There is no moment when a pause isn't an active gesture. No moment when everything isn't happening. The alchemy of a spot is not so exact as to be four elements equally spread out, but is a gentle thing, swayed from season to season, from water, to fire, to earth, to air—and then of course, there is the fifth element. This fifth element is what emits silence. The fifth element is spirit and is everything, yet nothing. Spirit is well-known yet has no recognizable scent. Its sound is common, yet has never been heard. It is as clear as seeing the Heron for the hundredth time, and at the same time as fresh as seeing a heron for the first time.

I suppose it's all really simple then. If in a pouring rainstorm we can stand and take comfort beneath a rookery of Heron nests, then for a brief moment all is as wise as a world in creation. All is steeped in primordial fluid, bloody as roots, old as the orders of angels, safe as good thoughts, sharp as quick scents.

*"Now the angel has come to earth and
the human has arrived in heaven."*
—Malcom Godwin

6. Swallowed Up While Observing

In the end I discover I have given myself to the Heron. Observers, without knowing how, will feel a slight bit of heat flush over their face, will shake their head and suddenly become aware that they have become the watched. This is the twist. To this reversal there is at once an end and a new unexpected beginning.

I set out merely to discover a place I was told about by a friend, because it sounded like a good adventure for the day. Quickly I became entrenched with fascination. After years of believing I was the one who was doing the watching, the studying and the understanding, I had my shudder of surprise. At some point, sitting still, watching, I felt a quivering, a gush of heat seep over me. I looked up wondering what had happened and saw the eyes of a Great Blue Heron, no more than twenty yards away, peering directly into me. When we matched eyes, I looked away first. I felt scared. Then, somehow, comforted. Worthy of being watched, not scary enough to fly from. This is perhaps a funny place to end the quest, but I am both exhausted and must recover from this gaze upon me. Never had I expected to become the observed. I know that all of this thinking about, watching and trying to understand Herons has taken me far, far away from where I started.

For now, the leaves have fallen off the sycamore trees, the young Herons have learned to fly and eat on their own. I straighten out my neck, tuck my soul into a nearby tree trunk and let myself rise up in the air, somewhere between earth and sky.

Prayers To Honor
The Great Blue Heron

Fire: Sacred flame. We respect your power and we present to you the Great Blue Heron, whom we care for, honor, love and respect. Please protect them and provide them with your good favor. We trust you to enlighten and enrich them with your sunlight, to give them needed energy, strength and courage. Let the blaze of your soul bring them growth, and may their passions be tended with care.

Water: Holy water, we present Great Blue Herons to you and ask that they never thirst, that the body of your life sustain them in every way. Let their flights be as flowing as you, ever changing, always sacred. At once rain and evaporation, then fog, then mist, now river lake or pond. Soon clouds, tides and creek.

Earth: Sacred earth, we thank you for your trees, wood, leaves. Honor and respect these Herons, keeping their bodies strong and whole. Let no harm come to them. Let them use your wise medicines when they encounter sickness. Provide them with the regenerative powers of growth. Know they use your earth wisely.

Air: Air all around us. Grant the Great Blue Herons your quickness when danger is near. Share your clear eyes for seeing, your ears for hearing, your way of discerning. May their breaths be clean and wholesome. Let their blood and their wings flow with your oxygen. When in your care, guide them safely in flight and migration.

Spirit: Deeply residing in the middle of all things, we ask you provide these birds with gratitude and faith. We know spirit is invisible, timeless, thick and enriched with the sweet elixir of bliss. Please Spirit, keep the Heron wedded to the earth, the water, the air, the fire.

There being a surprising lack of material written on the life and habits of the Great Blue Heron, I list the sources I used to bolster my observations, in no particular order.

Paul Shepard, *Man in the Landscape*
Gary Snyder, *The Practice of the Wild*
Barry Lopez, *Of Wolves and Men*
Robert Butler, *The Great Blue Heron*
Hayward Allen, *The Great Blue Heron*
Shierry Nicolsen-Weber,
    The Love of Nature and the End of the World
Thomas Roszak, *The Voice of the Earth*
Sir James Fraser, *The Golden Bough*
Sara Maitland, *A Joyful Theology*
David Abram, *Spell of the Sensuous*
Derrick Jensen, *A Language Older Than Words*
Malcom Godwin, *Angels*
Allan Megill, *Prophets of Extremity*
Aldo Leopold, *Sand County Almanac*
Belden Lane,
    Geography of the Sacred
    Fierce Landscapes
Terry Tempest Williams, *Coyote's Canyon*
Jorge Luis Borges
    Collected Fictions
    Collected Non-fictions
E.F. Schumacher, *A Guide for the Perplexed*
Gary Holthaus, *Wide Skies*
Bishop Kallistos Ware, *The Orthodox Way*
Edward Abbey, *Desert Solitaire*
Robert Wolf, *The Triumph of Technique*
Marnie Reed Crowell, *Great Blue: The Oydessy of a*
    Great Blue Heron
Joe Napora, *Flight of the Heron*

Additional praise for
The Great Blues

"This slim volume devoted to heron-awareness is a pleasure to hold as well as read."
—*The Iowa Source*

"I've been becoming more and more impatient wondering where nature writing might go next. *The Great Blues* has helped me think about this with what feels like greater clarity. Mythological natural history is at least as useful—and perhaps a lot more useful—than scientifically derived natural history for writing about another species."
—*Peter Sauer*

"A Kansas naturalist knows he has stumbled into a magical world where natural history and mythology are one."
—*Orion*

"I find myself thinking about this book, even though it's been months since I read it. Sometime before spring, I will read it again. And when I spot the first heron next summer, I'll be prepared to be crazy too."
—*Wapsipinicon Almanac*

Steve Semken is the founder of the Ice Cube Press which began in 1993 along the shores of the Kaw River in North Lawrence, Kansas. The press is now located in North Liberty, Iowa (www.icecubepress.com). He is the author of several books dealing with the natural world. His debut novel, *Pick Up Stick City*, was released by River's Bend Press, Stillwater, Minnesota. He has been Directer of the Standing By Words Center since 1998 (www.standingbywords.org).

Andrew R. Driscoll is an Assistant Professor of Art at Baker University. He lives in Lawrence, Kansas with his wife Kelly and their three children.

www.ingramcontent.com/pod-product-compliance
Lightning Source LLC
Chambersburg PA
CBHW031900170626
46807CB00004B/1815